MR. NOSEY
and the big surprise

Original concept by Roger Hargreaves
Illustrated and written by Adam Hargreaves

MR. MEN   LITTLE MISS

MR. MEN™ LITTLE MISS™ © THOIP (a Sanrio company)

Mr. Nosey and the big surprise © 1998 THOIP (a Sanrio company)
Printed and published under licence from Price Stern Sloan, Inc., Los Angeles.
This edition published in 2014 by Dean, an imprint of Egmont UK Limited,
The Yellow Building, 1 Nicholas Road, London W11 4AN

ISBN 978 0 6035 6774 2
54183/2
Printed in Great Britain

All rights reserved. No part of this publication may be reproduced, stored in a retrieval system, or transmitted,
in any form or by any means, electronic, mechanical, photocopying, recording or otherwise, without the
prior permission of the publisher and copyright owner.

Mr Nosey is the sort of person who does not mind his own business.

He minds everyone else's business!

He is as nosey as his nose is long.

If there is a keyhole to look through or a letter box to listen at you'll find Mr Nosey there looking or listening, and probably both.

One day while Mr Nosey was taking a walk through the wood on the other side of Tiddletown he heard a door shut.

"That's odd," he said to himself.

Mr Nosey peered around a tree and there was a wall. A wall that he had never noticed before.

Now, Mr Nosey can't go past a wall without knowing what is on the other side.

And rather handily this wall had a door in it. A small yellow door.

Mr Nosey being the nosey fellow he is could not resist taking a look.

He opened the door and peered around it.

On the other side of the wall was a tiny house with a yellow door.

Inside the house was a lift.

Mr Nosey got in the lift and pressed the button.

The lift went down.

And down.

And down.

And down, for what seemed like a very long time.

At the bottom the lift doors opened onto a long tunnel with a light at the end.

Mr Nosey set off down the tunnel.

By this time Mr Nosey was very curious.

He couldn't wait to see where the tunnel would lead.

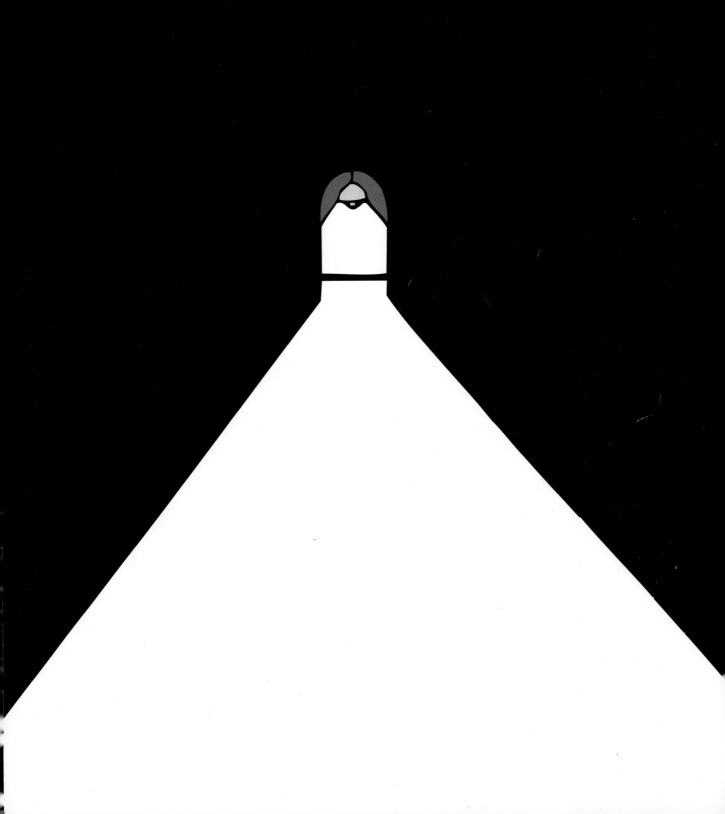

At the end of the tunnel there was another small yellow door.

And then another tunnel.

"There must be something really interesting at the end," Mr Nosey said to himself, as he hurried along.

He came to another door and then a long, winding staircase and another tunnel at the top.

Mr Nosey had quite lost track of time but he felt sure that he was coming close to the end.

He finally came to yet another small, yellow door just like all the others ... except this one had a keyhole.

Mr Nosey peeked through the keyhole.

All he could see was a white room, so he opened the door and there was a white room.

Nothing else!

No furniture.

No carpets.

No pictures.

Just a white room.

Mr Nosey walked into the room.

He had never been so disappointed in all his life.

He turned to leave and it was then that he saw a note stuck to the back of the door.

And written on the note was:

TEE! HEE!

SIGNED: Mr Mischief

Mr Nosey groaned.

And went home ... the long way.

And now you know what to do if you ever discover a small, yellow door.

Keep walking!

MR. NOSEY
and the big surprise

Mr Nosey likes to know everyone's business. He's always looking through keyholes and listening at letterboxes. But what will Mr Nosey discover behind the yellow door in the woods?

www.mrmen.com

£5.99

egmont.co.uk

ISBN 978-0-6035-6774-2

DEAN

9 780603 567742

LITTLE MISS NEAT
and the last leaf

Roger Hargreaves